Fingerprints A

W9-AJO-267

Without his best friend it was a lonely summer for Joachim. Everything he did seemed to lead to trouble—like the time he got stuck in the chicken coop, or the time he wanted to look in Gubben Janson's beehives. Joachim couldn't help being curious. He was only trying to find out how things worked, and mechanical things were the most fascinating of all.

Next door was the watchmaker's house, taunting him every day. He wanted so very much to see inside, to learn the mysterious workings of watches. If only there were a way. . . .

This is a sensitive story of an in-between time in the life of a Swedish boy.

A Time for Watching

A Time
for Watching

by Gunilla Norris

Illustrated by Paul Giovanopoulos

Alfred A. Knopf: New York

For my nephew, Bradford,
because he is a boy's boy,
and for my dear nieces,
Susanna and Faith

Contents

A Time for Watching

Chapter One

✛

Greta's Doll

It was awful. His whole summer was ruined. Why did Olle, his best and only friend, have to go off to spend the summer with his grandparents? Joachim Magnuson kicked up dust in the road. In the fifteen houses on this side of the village Olle was the only other boy. Now there were just girls left, and two of them were his sisters. Joachim grimaced and looked far down the gravel road at the village.

It looked like so many others in the Kopparberg district of Sweden, full of small red houses with painted white trim. In the center of town were the few stores, all crowded together on the main street. Only beyond the stores, on the other side of town, were there some boys. But Anders, Erik, and Sverker and their friends stuck together like burs; there was no hope being friends with them. Joachim shrugged. He didn't want to be friends with them anyway. They had to do everything in a pack, as if they couldn't breathe separately.

He liked to do things alone with Olle, like catching insects, exploring, and pasting up their stamp collections. But now . . . Joachim ground his heels in the dirt. Now there was nothing to do but his chores.

Slowly Joachim went around to the back of his house to the vegetable patch. Angrily he yanked at the weeds. Mamma and Papa didn't understand either. They just kept blaming him for getting into trouble. He was only finding out about things—like Mr. Kjellgren's lawnmower or Mamma's coffee mill. And when he did, it made him feel less lonely, as if for a minute he had discovered something exciting he could tell Olle about in the fall.

Fall, and another school year, was months away. By fall he would be almost eleven. Joachim sighed and wiped his face with the back of his muddy hands. Wistfully he looked across to Gubben Janson's house next to his own.

If only he could get the watchmaker to talk to him. Really talk. Or if he could just get inside the old man's house. Then he'd have something truly exciting to tell Olle. Getting inside that house had been Olle's and his dream ever since they were little boys. But it was hopeless. He knew that. No child had been allowed in that house since before the war began. And now the war was over.

Joachim stood up. He couldn't stand weeding anymore. Somehow sitting there in the vegetable garden made him think of Olle and what they always did in the summer—swimming in Mr. Kjellgren's brook and building forts in the woods behind Mrs. Grundling's house.

Joachim's mouth turned down. He couldn't weed all summer, could he? He had to do something, something to keep his mind off Olle and the long lonely summer days ahead. But everything he thought was interesting lately got him into trouble. Well, he couldn't stand to weed another second. Joachim threw a clod of dirt into the cabbage sprouts. He would at least go inside.

Joachim trudged to the house. Automatically he went and washed his hands. He made his way to his room slowly. As he passed, he looked into his little sister's room. Joachim stopped. Something caught his eye. Of course, that was just the thing. He slipped into the kitchen to make sure he would be safe. Yes, his little sister Greta was there with Mamma. They were making cookies. Fortunately, Karin, his older sister, wasn't home. Now was the time. If he worked swiftly, Greta would never know.

Quickly Joachim tiptoed into his little sister's room. He slid the door shut. Greta's doll was tucked into the bed. Joachim snatched up the blue-eyed baby, and it cried out, "Mamma," as if in protest. Joachim stopped. He held his breath. Would Greta hear her favorite calling? Joachim listened, but only soft kitchen noises reached him. He breathed a little easier.

With the doll tucked under his shirt he scurried to his room and shut the door. Now he could find out about the noise mechanism inside the doll. He'd been dying to know about it ever since Greta first got the doll. Now he was going to find out for himself and for Olle. He would only open the doll, look at the noise box, and put it all back together again. All he was interested in was the noise box.

Mamma and Papa wouldn't understand, though. No one understood except Olle. Joachim snorted. It seemed that as long as things worked, grownups didn't care about *how* they worked.

"Don't touch it!"

"Joachim, I need that!"

"You've got no right to touch someone else's things!"

"When will you ever think about other people?"

Lately Mamma and Papa had been going on and on, worse than ever. Joachim shook his head. How could they look at something and not want to know about nuts and screws and bolts and gears? Why, he bet there wasn't a grownup in the village, even in the whole district of Kopparberg, who cared about machines. Except, of course, Gubben Janson. But he was hopeless. You couldn't get near him even though he was just next door. Joachim sighed.

But now he had the doll to work on. Soon he would know. All he had to do was open the doll and find out.

Joachim made a space on his littered desk. He brushed the heavy brown hair away from his eyes and inspected the doll. There was a seam in the back. That was the place to cut it open. Joachim opened his pocketknife. He began cutting. He'd have to do it carefully so that he could get it back together. Whoops! His hand slipped and the knife slanted. It made a little cut into the body of the doll. Well, it didn't matter. It was just a doll, after all, even if Greta didn't think so.

Now the hole was big enough. Something shone in there. Joachim thrust his quick long fingers into the doll and brought out a little metal box. So that was what it looked like. Joachim turned it in his agile hand. "Mamma," yelled the box. "Mamma." It was funny hearing the box yell. Joachim laughed. Olle would have thought it was funny too.

But what made the noise? His sharp eyes looked the box over. He would have to open it. If he was really careful, nothing would go wrong. "Mamma," whimpered the box as he laid it on the desk. In a few moments he had all the pieces in order on the inkstained blotter. Joachim sighed, looking at all the little parts. So that was how it was made. He and Olle would never have guessed. . . .

The door opened. Greta stood looking at the desk, wide-eyed and suspicious. When she saw the doll, she began to cry in long wailing hiccups.

"Shhhh! Greta, come on," said Joachim. "It's only a doll. I was very careful. I'll have it together soon. Just be quiet."

But Greta would not be quiet. She cried louder still.

"Stop it!" hissed Joachim, trying to put the voice box together again as fast as he could.

Then Mamma came. "What is it?" she asked. Then she saw.

"No, Joachim," she said sadly. "You didn't. Not Greta's favorite doll. How could you?"

"It's only a doll," said Joachim defiantly.

"But, Joachim, look at Greta. Don't you see how she feels?"

"She's acting like a baby," he said.

"No, Joachim," said Mamma. "You're ten, but this summer you're the one who is acting like a baby, following your whims, taking others' things without a thought about their feelings."

"But I was careful. I'll have it back together again . . . "

"You'll stay right in here," said Mamma, "until that doll is fixed and until Papa comes home. Is that understood?"

"Yes," said Joachim wearily.

Then Mamma took Greta in her arms and shut the door behind her.

Chapter Two

The Coal Chute

It had happened again. Nobody understood. Nobody wanted to understand. Joachim was sure Papa would come home and take Greta's side. He was always on the side of "other" people. What did he do all day but sell stamps in the post office and listen endlessly to everybody else's troubles? Well, Joachim had some troubles, too; like being in the middle between two sisters, like having Olle away for the summer, and like being right next door to a person like Gubben Janson.

Joachim sighed and pressed his nose to the window. His house was on the dusty road just outside the main part of town. It was a small, red, one-storied house with a little porch flanked by two benches. Gubben Janson's house was exactly the same, but instead of having starched organdy curtains and geraniums in

the windows the old man had shutters—closed shutters.

Gubben Janson was the most unusual grownup Joachim knew. He was a beekeeper and, better still, a watchmaker. So many times Joachim and Olle had tried to get the old man to talk to them, only to be shooed away. Gubben Janson hated children. Once long ago some child had made mischief in the old man's house and had broken two precious clocks. He had never forgotten it. Now he would sit on his front porch and yell at everyone under twelve.

"You've got itchy fingers. Go home. Scat!" And then he'd poke his walking stick at them in the air.

Three times Joachim had been poked in the back when he hadn't gone home. Now he did what all the children did when they passed Gubben Janson's house. They went behind it through the fields, or they crawled on their hands and knees in the ditch on the opposite side of the road. Of course, when Gubben Janson was inside repairing watches, they could walk right down the main road. But crawling in the ditch was beginning to be a habit for most of the children living in the village.

Joachim left the window and sat down by the desk. He began assembling the voice box. With everything in place it did not take very long. But it only said, "Ma," now. Joachim tried to make it say "Mamma," but no matter what he tried, it would not do it. Discouraged, Joachim put the box down. He looked at it angrily. He wanted to make it work right. Why wouldn't it? Gubben Janson would know what to do. Much good that did!

He went to the window again and looked out. There was the old man's house full of tools and machines. Full of things he and Olle would love. Why didn't the old man want to share what he knew? Joachim would sneak into the house if he could, but Gubben Janson was very agile for an old man. He didn't see very well anymore, but he could hear a fly on the wall, and he could move quickly with that walking stick of his.

Joachim put the faulty voice box back in the doll. Carefully he sewed up the seam in the doll's back and the rip where the knife had slanted off the mark. There! He turned the toy over. "Ma!" it groaned. Well, Greta would have to be happy with it. He had done his best, and he couldn't do better.

But Greta was not happy with the doll, and Papa, when he came home, was not happy with Joachim.

"Joachim," Papa said, "what has come over you lately? Why won't you leave other people's things alone? When will you think about somebody else?"

Joachim looked down. Papa didn't understand. With him it was always "other people." Other people. Other people. He was all alone, and nobody cared about him. Papa cared about other people, and Gubben Janson, the only grownup who could possibly understand, didn't care for anybody. Joachim went to his room and slammed the door.

From the moment summer vacation began, it had been like this. Without Olle everything seemed dull—the insect collection, the stamps—everything. Everything seemed dull now except the inside of Gubben Janson's house.

If only he could get into the old man's house. That would really be something to tell about. He looked at the house across the way. The shutters were closed, just as the old man was closed against him. If only there were some way. . . . Joachim looked longingly past the old man's beehives behind the house.

Suddenly Joachim straightened up. What was that? He flattened his nose to the glass to see better. Why hadn't he noticed that before? There was an opening to the house—the coal chute. It had a swinging metal door. Maybe that was a way. Maybe. But no . . . Joachim didn't dare. The old man would hear him. But what if he made no noise at all? Joachim shook his head. He did not want to feel the old man's walking stick again. But then . . .

Chapter Three

⊹

Joachim Practices

Joachim could not get the coal chute out of his mind. It popped into his head while he did the weeding or when he beat the rugs free of dust on cleaning day. Then his black eyes had a faraway look. Mamma shook her head and hoped her son was not up to anything new.

Joachim kept thinking about the coal chute and how big the opening was and wondering whether he wouldn't just fit through. He was a short boy for his age, thin and wiry, although he ate at least two helpings of everything. Maybe if he skipped second helpings for a while, he would get thinner and would be able to slide through the coal chute door the way wet soap slid through his hands. Abruptly, Joachim decided to stop eating, and his mother worried more.

"Joachim," she said, "what's on your mind, dear? Why aren't you eating the lovely sponge cake? Is something wrong?"

"Oh, no, Mamma. I'm not hungry," lied Joachim and stared across his freckled nose.

"I wish you'd tell me," she said gently, "before anything goes wrong."

But Joachim did not hear. In his mind he was sneaking up behind Gubben Janson's house without a fear. Wait till he told Olle!

Mamma gave him a good wake-up shake and a gentle kiss.

"Well, then," she declared, "you must go outside and work up an appetite."

Joachim was terribly hungry as it was. He did not need to work up an appetite at all. In fact, he had to do something to keep his mind off sponge cake and *plättar*, the pancakes he heaped with lingonberry sauce, and meat with lots of fried onions. There was only one thing that could replace food right now—Gubben Janson's coal chute. But Gubben Janson was sitting on the front porch with both ears wide open and the walking stick between his knees.

Joachim went out and took the ditch way past his house and came out near Lundkvist's Konditori. He met Anders and Erik on the way, but they were so busy with each other that they didn't even say hello. Joachim frowned and stared at the bakery window. It was amazing how sponge cake kept popping up in front of him; there was a great big one displayed in the window.

No. Joachim pulled himself away from the bakery window and wandered down the gravel road past the post office, where he waved to his father, and past the kiosk, where the advertisements beckoned to him with their chocolatey invitations to buy. Joachim dragged himself away until he was almost outside town.

At Mr. Kjellgren's farm the chickens were strutting and pecking around their pen and their hen house. As Joachim watched, he noticed that the swinging door of the hen house was almost as big as the door to Gubben Janson's coal chute.

Quickly he unlatched the wire gate of the pen and went inside. As he looked more closely at the swinging door, he felt sure. It was perfect to practice on. He could find out right now whether he was thin enough.

Joachim lay down on the ground and put his head into the hen house through the door. It smelled of chickens, and the noise was terrific. The hens inside set up a fearful squawking and went right up to him, scolding and pecking at him.

"I'm not a hen," said Joachim soothingly to the chickens. "Don't get excited." He pulled himself further into the hen house, and then his shoulders caught painfully in the door. He lay still for a while. This reminded him of something his mother had read to him when he was little. Oh, yes, Winnie-the-Pooh getting stuck in a tight place and all the friends coming.

Joachim grunted. The chickens certainly were not friendly.

18

"Scat! Go away!" he said. He dug his toes into the yard and tried to push himself inside.

Squawk, squawk went the chickens. They were noisier than ever. Then he felt someone yanking on his legs.

"Joachim Magnuson, get out of there," said a very stern voice.

Joachim froze. It was Mr. Kjellgren. Joachim felt his legs being pulled, and out of the hen house he popped like a jack in the box. His brown hair was covered with dust and chicken feathers.

"Explain this," said Mr. Kjellgren, looking very angry. "You've left the gate to the chicken pen open. Most of the hens are out on the road now. And you've disturbed my best layers in the hen house."

Joachim looked away.

"Well? What do you have to say for yourself?"

"I'm . . . I'm sorry. I . . . ." He couldn't tell Mr. Kjellgren that he was practicing getting through Gubben Janson's coal chute!

"If you haven't anything to say, I'm afraid I'll have to talk to your mother," said Mr. Kjellgren. "Last week you tinkered with my lawnmower, and before that it was something else. You've caused me enough trouble, even if you are Postman Magnuson's boy. Why don't you play with your friends instead of being a nuisance?"

"Yes, sir," said Joachim sullenly. How could he play with Olle

20

when he was away? Could he help it if there was no one else he liked?

"Come along now. You'd better learn to stay out of my things."

Joachim bit his lip. Silently he helped Mr. Kjellgren herd the chickens back into the pen. One hen was missing.

"See what you've done?" said Mr. Kjellgren. "It's got to stop."

Mr. Kjellgren took Joachim by the collar and firmly escorted him home. Joachim waited outside while Mr. Kjellgren went inside to tell Mamma what had happened. Joachim sat down heavily on the front porch, trying not to think of anything at all. But he knew what was going to happen. The grownup solution for everything lately was a licking. If only he could explain. But what was the use? Only Olle would understand. Joachim waited gloomily. There it was, his mother's call.

"Joachim Magnuson, come in here."

Joachim gulped slowly. "Yes, Mamma. I'm coming."

"I'm going to have to punish you," she said sternly.

Joachim didn't say anything. He just stretched out over a chair. Smack went the willow stick on his bottom. Smack! Smack!

It stung awfully, and for a minute Joachim had a hard time keeping the tears back.

"That's enough," said Mamma, and she sounded relieved that it was over. "Please say something to Mr. Kjellgren."

"I'm sorry," mumbled Joachim. But he was not sorry. What

did one little chicken matter? He rubbed the seat of his pants. He must not cry. He was too big for that.

"I'm sorry, too," said Mamma. She sat down on the wooden bench. "I don't understand," she said as she wiped her eyes on her flowered apron. "I just don't understand."

Chapter Four

Joachim Listens

Joachim had to go to bed early. He crawled into his wooden bed, which was built right into the wall. He pulled the red blanket over his head to make it dark so he could sleep. But the light from the window still came into his room. It told of a long bright evening, a summer evening that Joachim had to spend alone in his room. The mattress felt lumpy under him as he tossed around. His stomach growled. He sat up. He began pacing on the strip of colorful rag rug. One . . . two . . . three . . . four steps, he was at one end. One . . . two . . . three . . . four, he was at the other. Back and forth he went. And then he heard voices. Softly he lifted the iron latch. Silently the door swung ajar.

His mother and father were talking in the rocking chairs by the window. Joachim guessed that Karin and Greta were outside.

"Gustav," said Mamma, "we must do something about Joachim. He's getting worse every day. I don't understand the boy lately. He gets that funny look in his eyes, and then something awful happens."

Joachim saw his father shake his head thoughtfully.

"I don't know what we are doing wrong," Mamma went on. "He doesn't seem to be able to stay out of trouble."

"I think you are making too much of it," said Papa. "Maybe it has something to do with Olle being away. Or maybe it's a sudden overdose of natural curiosity. In time, with proper discipline, he'll learn to control it."

"But Gustav," said Mamma, "he's always in trouble now. He doesn't think about people. Perhaps if you could speak to him, if you could put his curiosity and his hands to work . . ."

"Well . . ."

"Gustav, couldn't you, couldn't you put him to work with you in the post office? Here he is only with girls. Perhaps if he were with you, perhaps if he felt that you cared about . . ."

"We can try," said Papa. "We can only try."

Joachim did not want to hear anymore. He closed the door and tiptoed over to his bed. He crawled under the sheet and the blanket. Somewhere deep inside he felt confused. He had never heard Mamma and Papa talking like that, especially Papa. Joachim bit his lip. He would try. He'd try to forget Gubben Janson. He'd try to forget the old man's house and all the marvelous things behind the white shutters.

Chapter Five

+

The Post Office Scale

The next morning at the breakfast table Joachim felt a bit strange and awkward. He did not look at his parents but slid into his painted chair silently. Then, as from a distance, he heard Papa say, "How about coming to the post office with me today, Joachim?"

Joachim looked up. "Fine," he said, trying to sound pleased and surprised at once. But it came out strangely.

"I could use a little help from my big boy," continued Papa. "We'll do some really good work."

Startled, Joachim looked at his father. Papa never talked like that. Joachim frowned.

"We'll be together the whole day," continued Papa, and Joachim saw him look at Mamma in an "Am I doing all right?"

sort of way. Joachim glanced quickly at Mamma. She was smiling, and the smile said, "Thank you, Gustav," plain as day. Joachim suddenly felt awful.

Why did they act like that? It was all pretend. Papa needed help like he needed three sets of legs. Last night he had felt . . . not really sorry . . . but different. But now . . . Joachim bent forward over his oatmeal. He would have to go with Papa, he knew that. There was nothing else to do.

"Are you trying to eat your oatmeal with your nose?" asked Karin, and Greta laughed.

"Girls!" snapped Papa and stood up. "Come on, Joachim, let's go."

They went out the dutch door and down the gravel road. The daisies bobbed in the wind near the ditches, and a barn swallow flew by. They walked silently. Then Joachim saw Mr. Kjellgren coming toward them.

"Hallo there, Magnuson!" said Mr. Kjellgren. "Going to keep close tabs on that son of yours today, I hope."

Papa laughed in an embarrassed way.

Joachim looked down at the gravel. His insides felt pinched and miserable. So that was what Papa had in mind—keeping close tabs so he would not have to be ashamed of him. Joachim bit his lip and closed his eyes while the men were talking. He could feel the early summer breeze across his face. He was not going to cry. He was not going to think about anything. He shut his eyes more tightly.

Then a vision of Gubben Janson's house sprang into his head. He imagined it whole and beautiful. In there were clocks and machines, wonderful constructions that couldn't care less about keeping tabs. That was the great thing Mamma and Papa didn't seem to know or care about. Machines never scolded or misunderstood or even felt. They whirred on comfortingly in their ordered ways. And Joachim longed to be with them, longed to know their secret workings.

"Joachim! Let's go. There's lots of work to do."

Joachim drifted back to the gravel road, to Mr. Kjellgren, and to the morning ahead. He shivered, and then silently he moved behind his father into the little post office.

"Now then," said Papa, "let's see where we'll put you to work." He looked around and scratched his head. "Where can we settle you?" Papa frowned as his eyes darted around the room. Then Joachim's face grew stiff. Now he knew it had all been pretend. Suddenly he couldn't stand it anymore. His black eyes flashed.

"You don't need help," he blurted out. "You're just trying to keep tabs on me like Mr. Kjellgren said."

"Joachim," said Papa, "that is no way to speak to your elders."

"You don't care," said Joachim, "as long as I'm not in trouble, as long as you don't have to be ashamed."

Papa looked hurt. "Whatever gave you that idea?"

"It's true!" cried Joachim.

"No, it's not true," said his father. "When you've calmed down, we'll talk about it. But right now there's no need for this conversation at all. Take the stool and sit at the back counter. I want you to weigh some letters.''

"Of course, he didn't want to talk about it!" thought Joachim. Sullenly he drew the high stool over to the counter.

"Here's the scale," said Papa. "Here are the letters. Write the weight on the right hand corner of the envelopes.''

Joachim was left alone. Slowly he climbed up on the stool and twisted his wiry legs around the rungs. He stared at the letters. He picked one up and flopped it onto the scale. The mechanism

jiggled. Slowly Joachim forgot the world around him. He watched the scale even out. If he had a screwdriver, he could find out what the scale looked like inside, how it was made. Silently he slid off the stool. His father was deep in conversation with a customer at the window. Joachim scurried around the post office. At last he found an old letter opener. It could serve as a screwdriver.

Slowly, painstakingly, he took the scale apart. There lay the vital parts all in order on the counter. To Joachim it was as though the world lay before him. There was the shaft, there were the balancing beam and the joint. He was so absorbed he didn't notice his father standing next to him.

"So," said Papa, "you have it apart. Now what?"

Joachim looked up. Suddenly he felt uncertain.

"Now what?" asked his father again.

"I can put it together," mumbled Joachim.

"That's not the point," said Papa.

Joachim looked down. He wanted to pull his head into his shirt, as if a storm were about to break just above him. But nothing happened.

Papa went over to the post office window and shut it.

"All right, Joachim," he said. "Look at me."

Joachim looked up uneasily.

"First, I'm glad you have an interest in machines and how they work. That's fine. But," Papa looked at him sternly, "I want you to listen carefully. If you are told to weigh letters, then weigh letters. I need that scale right now. It has worked perfectly well for me. I have to get some packages off on the next mail car. I promised they would be on it."

"I'll have it together soon," said Joachim.

"But you had no right in the first place to take the scale apart without permission," said Papa.

"The packages can go with the next car," said Joachim defiantly.

"Yes, they can. But it means I've broken a promise just waiting for you to put that scale together."

"I was right," said Joachim. "You don't care about me. You don't care about how things work or anything." Somehow it didn't matter what he said. Joachim felt angry and empty.

"Listen, Joachim," said Papa. "Would I be cross if I didn't care about things? I care that the scale is all in pieces. I care that you disobeyed my instructions. I care what you do to other people."

Joachim looked at his scuffed shoes. What was the use? All Papa wanted was the mail scale to work and Joachim not to annoy anyone. He only cared about *not* being ashamed.

"Joachim," his father put a hand on his shoulder.

Joachim winced and looked away.

"I don't know everything in your head. You're probably feeling pretty misunderstood. But why don't you try to do some of your own understanding?"

Joachim knew he was expected to answer. All he wanted to do was to leave and bang the door.

32

"All right?" his father asked.

Joachim gave as small a nod as possible.

"That's good," sighed Papa. "Now let's see you put the scale together."

Slowly Joachim looked up at the counter. There was the scale spread out with its secret parts exposed. It was worth every bit of scolding. Those parts were beautiful. Joachim touched them gently. He would tell Olle all about them.

Chapter Six

+

A Strange Mailing

The next day Joachim again walked silently behind his father to the post office. They hadn't talked much, though Papa had looked startled and pleased when the mail scale was back together again.

"That's fine," he had said, and Joachim had felt satisfied. But now there was nothing left to fix or take apart.

Joachim set to work sorting mail, putting letters in the heavy gray canvas bags. His father was busy at the window selling stamps and weighing packages. Joachim felt listless. It was such dull work, and it was not even noon when he ran out of letters to sort. There was nothing to do.

His father had no time because he was busy talking to his customers. They all stopped to chat of this and that. Papa always asked about everybody. How was Mrs. Grundling's leg? And how were Mr. Kjellgren's hens? On and on it went. Papa never seemed to get tired of it. In fact, people came whether they had mail or not.

Joachim couldn't understand what was so interesting about talking all day. He grew sleepy, and it was all he could do to keep his eyes open. Then finally Papa looked at his watch. It had stopped. He shook it gently.

"My watch has stopped," he said. "Wonder what time it is? The mail car should be coming soon. But I need to get home to fetch my order slips."

Joachim peered sleepily at his father.

"Can you take care of things here?" he asked.

Joachim nodded.

"I'm trusting you, Joachim," said Papa in that "better not get into trouble" tone of voice. "When the mail car comes, there are just those two canvas bags to go."

"Yes, all right," said Joachim and felt a little bit put out. His father couldn't trust him even for a minute.

It was a relief to be alone at last. The flies buzzed lazily. Only one or two landed on the curl of sticky flypaper at the window. Joachim looked around. He'd show Papa. He wasn't going to touch a thing. There were two mailbags full and a big empty one. He picked up the empty one and looked inside. Joachim decided to get into it. There, at least, he couldn't touch anything.

He pulled the flap of the bag over his head with satisfaction. It was warm inside. He could take a snooze and then he would be sure to stay out of trouble. Besides, no one would come now, when it was almost lunch time. Before long Joachim fell asleep, and the flies went on buzzing lazily.

When the mail car came the driver picked up three canvas bags, securing the locks on all three flaps. He wondered a little where Postman Magnuson was and why there was so much extra mail. But he didn't think much more about it. With the bags safely in the back of the car, he drove off to the next village.

Joachim woke up with a start. The bag had grown stuffy. His father would soon be back. But when he tried to crawl out of the bag, he found the flap stuck. Joachim kicked furiously against the canvas. What was happening? He kicked again and again until he grew tired. And then slowly he sensed that he was in motion, and the whole situation became clear to him. He was in the mail car in a mailbag. He had mailed himself, and no one was left to tend the post office.

Joachim's heart sank. He had done something again. Why, *why* couldn't he just have left the mailbag alone? And how was he ever to get out of it?

The mail car came to a stop. Joachim called and called, but the idling motor growled noisily, and the driver did not hear. Instead, two more bags landed on top of Joachim, and the car started up again. Joachim had to make the best of it and wait for the car to reach the post office in Falun. He groaned under the weight of the written word and felt like crying.

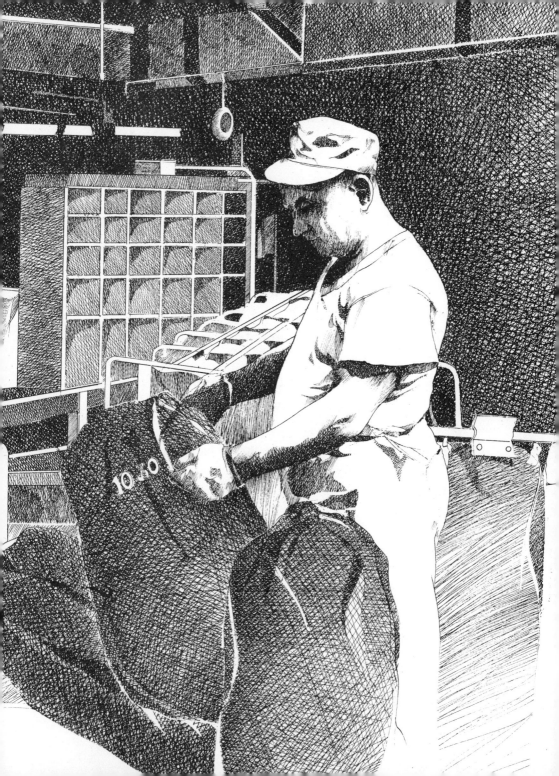

At last the car stopped again. Joachim heard the door open. Two of the bags were lifted off. He could move again.

"Help!" he cried and stirred in the bag. "Get me out!"

The driver was dumbfounded. "I must be hearing things," he mumbled.

"Help!" yelled Joachim and kicked at the canvas.

"Well, I'll be strapped and paddled," said the driver. Quickly he undid the flap of Joachim's bag. And there was Joachim's face, red as a boiled crayfish from the heat of the canvas.

"So that was the extra heavy mailing," laughed the driver. "I'll be. And who are you?"

"Joachim Magnuson," mumbled Joachim, feeling stripped down to the bare skin.

"Glad to meet you," chuckled the driver. "It's lucky I have to take the evening run. You can ride home in the mail car. But what your father will say, that's another story."

It wasn't what his father would say that Joachim worried about but what he would do.

But when he got home, his father did not do anything. Joachim could tell Mamma and Papa had worried about him. They just looked at him drearily, and that was worse. Joachim went to his room on his own and went to bed without supper.

Chapter Seven

✛

Joachim Goes to Gubben Janson's House

The next day it rained. Rain poured over the berry patch and Gubben Janson's beehives. It poured into the ditch and into the rain barrels. Joachim moved around the house restlessly. He was sorry about what had happened yesterday, but at breakfast his mother did not mention it, and Papa just read the paper silently.

But Greta and Karin had plenty to say.

"Chicken boy. Squawk! Squawk!" cried Greta, imitating Mr. Kjellgren's hens.

"Mailbag! Mailbag!" said Karin, joining in the fun, even though Joachim thought she was too old for that at fourteen. He kept his lips closed and shut his ears. But it was hard.

To console himself he asked for a cookie, but Mamma said they were all for the midsummer fair for the Red Cross. Joachim sighed and went to his room. His father had gone to the post office alone. Joachim didn't know what to feel—relief or disappointment. It was all mixed up together. Papa had not seemed angry at breakfast, only awfully quiet as if he were thinking. Joachim did not know what it meant.

He sighed and looked at his stamp collection. The solemn faces of kings looked back at him. Their faces were either blue or green or pink. Without Olle it wasn't any fun. Joachim put the stamps away, and all the while the thought of Gubben Janson's house kept coming back. He felt fretful and angry with himself. He tried to fix an old mechanical toy, but he gave up because he did not have the right tools, not like the ones Gubben Janson must have.

Then Greta began again. "Joachim! Chicken Kim!"

"Stop!" roared Joachim.

And then Karin joined in. "Mailbag! Mailbag!"

Joachim was so angry that he went to his sister's room, picked the lock of her treasure box, and took a letter at random.

"My dearest love," he recited as loudly as possible, "I love you like the sky, like the moon and stars, like the forget-me-nots in spring . . ."

He did not get very far, because Karin snatched the letter away and hit him in the stomach.

"Children! Children!" said Mamma in exasperation. "Stop now. It's almost lunch time. Why isn't Papa here yet? He's been late for two days now."

"Oh, he's always hearing everybody's news. It goes on and on. Besides, I think his watch is broken," mumbled Joachim.

"Then we'll have to have it fixed."

Joachim stopped. If the watch had to be fixed, someone had to take it to Gubben Janson. And that someone would be a customer and would go inside the house. Suddenly Joachim felt terribly excited.

"Mamma, may I take the watch to Gubben Janson? Please!"

"I thought all the children were afraid of Gubben Janson," said Mamma, looking at him carefully.

"We are," said Joachim. "But please, may I take the watch?"

Mrs. Magnuson looked at her son.

"Please, Mamma."

"We'll talk to Papa," she said, softened by Joachim's eagerness.

When Papa came home for lunch at last, Joachim was at the door.

"May I take your watch to Gubben Janson, Papa? It needs fixing. Please, may I?"

"Well now," said Papa and looked at Joachim's eager face. "It's true that the watch has stopped. But I thought it best to have it repaired in Falun. The mail driver could take it on one of his runs."

"But why?" cried Joachim.

"Well, it's just that Gubben Janson is getting old, and his eyesight is growing poor. I guess that's why he's getting slower and slower each year. And then, too, it's as if he only cares for the watches—never mind the people who need them. Why he's been repairing Mrs. Grundling's grandfather clock for six months."

"Maybe there is a lot wrong with it," said Joachim.

"Maybe. But I think he just likes having everybody's watches around so he can tinker with them. I can't wait that long."

"Please, Papa," said Joachim. "I could take it. I'd be careful."

"Gustav," said Mamma softly, "perhaps it wouldn't be such a bad idea."

"But to wait four months for him to finish . . . I don't think I could do that. Mr. Kjellgren has taken his kitchen clock to the city. He felt he couldn't wait either."

"Oh, please," cried Joachim.

"Hmmmm," said Papa looking at Joachim's disappointed face. "Maybe it wouldn't hurt to be without a watch for a while. I guess you may take it. But tell him it's a rush job."

"I will," said Joachim. His face beamed gratefully at Papa. "I will right now."

Watch in hand, Joachim went to Gubben Janson's house. His heart beat quickly. Surely the old man wouldn't strike at him. He was there on real business. He clutched the watch in his hand.

Joachim rapped on the door. He knew Gubben Janson was inside because it was raining. And afraid as he was, he was certain that at last he would see the inside of Gubben Janson's house. Now he would really have something to tell Olle.

Joachim rapped on the door again. Finally, something stirred and the door opened a crack.

"Go away," said the old man peering at Joachim through the crack. "Don't bother me."

"But, sir, I have my father's watch, and it needs fixing. Please may I come in?"

"Let me see," said Gubben Janson and stuck out a gnarled hand. Joachim put the watch in it. But that was a mistake, because as soon as the watch changed hands, Gubben Janson closed the door and threw the latch with a bang.

Joachim stood there dumbfounded. He hadn't even had a chance to say it was a rush job. Joachim raised his hand to rap on the door, but he knew it was no use.

Dejectedly Joachim went home.

"Well," asked Papa, "what did he say?"

"He just snatched the watch from my hand," mumbled Joachim.

"Without as much as a how-do-you-do?" asked Mamma.

"No, nothing. I didn't even have a chance to tell him we needed it back soon."

"Well, what did I say?" remarked Papa irritably. "It isn't your fault, Joachim, but it's goodbye watch for six months."

But Joachim did not hear him. He was thinking goodbye something else—goodbye to seeing the inside of Gubben Janson's house, now or ever.

Chapter Eight

⊹

The Midsummer Fair

Midsummer Day broke cold and overcast.

"Oh, dear," said Mamma at breakfast, "I hope we'll still have customers at the bazaar, even though it is a dreadful day."

Greta was grumpy. "If it rains, there won't be a puppet show," she said, and her lips twitched already with disappointment.

"Now, now, go outside," said Mamma. "If there is enough blue between the clouds to make a pair of overalls, we'll be all right. Go and look."

Greta ran outside. Between the low-hanging clouds was a small patch of blue sky. A little tiny patch. Greta came into the house shivering.

"There's only enough blue for a pair of overalls for my doll," she said gloomily.

"That isn't much. But it's something," said Mamma. "Karin, why don't you take Greta to the fairground and watch the raising of the maypole?"

Karin said no, she would rather stay home and read about Katinka. The book was just getting good. Katinka had just fallen in love with the mysterious stranger.

"Well then, Joachim, will you please take Greta?" asked Mamma.

Joachim looked up. The last thing he wanted was to have Greta in tow, but something inside made him nod anyway.

Mamma looked startled. Then she beamed at him. "Thank you, Joachim," she said giving him a swift kiss. "That's a real help."

They started out, passing Gubben Janson's house by the ditch way and cutting off toward the fairground. The fairground was always Mr. Kjellgren's big field. He had cut his first crop of hay just in time for the festivities.

There were the men about to raise the maypole. It had been dressed by the women of the village with leaves and field flowers from top to bottom, as had the cross pieces. On each arm hung a large garland of dog roses and daisies and clover. Already the ropes for the raising were tied to the pole. The men stood ready.

"One . . . two . . . three . . . hey!" Up went the maypole waving above the field, and down it sank again. Joachim held his breath. He knew it was hard to raise such a large thing.

"One . . . two . . . three . . . hey!" Up flew the pole, and this time down went the base of it into the open hole in the middle

of the field. It was a very deep hole. Quickly the men secured the maypole, filling in the rest of the hole and bracing the maypole itself. It stood tall and majestic, sprouting leaves and flowers like a tree from the first garden.

All around the fairground booths were being hammered together: one for lemonade, one for cakes and goodies, one for hot dogs, one for darts, one for the wet sponge game—and the puppet stage was just being finished.

"Look, Joachim," said Greta. "There *was* enough blue in the sky. The puppet stage is up. Oh, thank you for bringing me."

Joachim smiled at Greta. He had been feeling a brisk breeze, and he saw the clouds tear apart like pieces of frayed cloth. The sun peered cautiously down on the fairground.

"It's going to be fine," chanted Greta. "It's going to be fine."

Under ordinary circumstances, Joachim would have been as excited as she, and he understood how she felt. But today he was still disappointed about yesterday. He had a nagging feeling of something unfinished. Besides, he thought he was getting a little old for ring dances and puppet shows.

After lunch the family dressed in their national costumes. Joachim and Papa wore caps, white shirts, and yellow knickers tied at the knees with laces sporting fat red pompons. Mamma and Karin and Greta wore wool skirts and laced bodices, striped aprons and little caps. Papa's and Mamma's costumes were old, handed down from their parents, but Joachim's and the girls' were recent hand-me-downs from some cousins in Morastrand.

The fairground was bursting with color. An accordion wheezed along with a squeaky violin and viola. They were familiar tunes: *Seven pretty girls in a ring* and *Mother's little pigs we are every one*. Circles formed around the maypole. The little children were closest and then the teenagers and then the old folk. Round and round they went, laughing and stamping. It made a royal business for the lemonade stand, because now the sun was beating down heartily, and the frayed clouds had become great white towers far off in the distance. Old and young alike ate and drank. Mrs. Magnuson kept time to the music with her feet behind the Red Cross booth. The cookies were disappearing quickly, and the change box felt heavy.

Joachim saw his father dancing a *hambo* with Mrs. Kjellgren, and Greta was watching one puppet beat another on the head. At the maypole Karin had a blissful look as she held hands with Baker Lundkvist's son.

Joachim sat under a tree. The festivities were going right by him. He didn't want to dance with any of the girls, and he had already eaten three hot dogs with plenty of Slotts mustard on them. He had spent all his leftover change on the wet-sponge game. The mail driver had volunteered to let his face be the target, and Joachim had hit him full in the nose with the sopping sponge three times. He had done better than Sverker or any of the other boys, too. But now there was nothing left to do.

Absently he watched a whirling butterfly near him. He had never seen that kind before. Joachim sat up. He could catch it for his collection. He got on his knees, ready to pounce, and then he saw something that drove butterflies from his mind.

Joachim's heart beat faster. His breath came quickly. He saw Gubben Janson walking briskly across the field with his walking stick in his hand. Behind him hurried Mrs. Grundling, trying to remind him about the grandfather clock. And there was Baker Lundkvist, buttonholing the old man and pointing to his own wrist.

Joachim watched a while as his mind raced on. If Gubben Janson was at the fairground, he was not at home. And if he was not at home . . . Joachim stood up. In a moment he had climbed over the fence of Mr. Kjellgren's field and left the fairground far behind him.

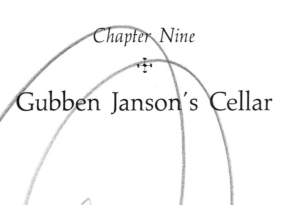

Chapter Nine

✠

Gubben Janson's Cellar

Joachim stopped in front of Gubben Janson's house and looked up and down the road. No one was coming. For a moment he hesitated. He knew he shouldn't do it. But it really wouldn't hurt anything. No one would know. They were all at the fairground.

Quickly Joachim tried the front door. It was locked, as was the back door. Joachim rounded the beehives, hearing the steady humming of the insects. In a moment he was by the coal chute. Kneeling down, he carefully lifted up the door. It was a good bit larger than the hen-house door. In went Joachim's feet. Down went his legs. Bigger door or not, it was a tight squeeze. Joachim was angry with himself for having eaten those three hot dogs. He pushed and grunted. At last his shoulders were through, and he slid down the chute to land with a bang in the coal bin. It was

frightfully dark. He stubbed his toe. He hit his head. But he was so excited he hardly noticed.

After a few minutes his eyes grew accustomed to the darkness. On the shelf he saw the dim outline of bee equipment: the netted hat Gubben Janson wore when the bees swarmed, gloves, and tools. And he saw what he was looking for, a rickety pair of stairs leading to the main house. Quickly Joachim climbed up. He tried the door. It was jammed. He shook the handle. He threw all his weight against the door. But it was locked. Joachim was so disappointed he wanted to cry.

There was nothing for him to do now but to climb out the way he had come. Slowly he made his way to the coal bin. He tried to walk up the coal chute, but he kept slipping back. And then he heard footsteps overhead. Joachim's heart stopped. Gubben Janson was back. What should he do? His foot caught on the side of the coal bin, and as he fell down, the coal rumbled under him. Upstairs the footsteps stopped. Somehow the coal dust had gotten into Joachim's nose. Try as he might, he could not hold back a sneeze.

"ATCH O O O O O O O O O O O O !" The sound echoed in the cellar. In a moment the door to the cellar opened. Down came Gubben Janson, moving more easily than anyone would have thought he could.

"You little rascal!" cried Gubben Janson. "So you found the coal chute." He raised the walking stick and stalked over to the coal bin. Joachim closed his eyes. His mouth felt terribly dry.

"I thought someone would find it one day," growled Gubben Janson. "That's why I made an automatic lock for the cellar door."

"Sir!" cried Joachim. "I'm sorry . . . I . . ."

The stick whined in the air. "I can't even go to the fairground without people threatening to take their business away. A man has no right to get older and slower, I suppose. Why I was mending clocks before they were born. They haven't an ounce of respect for delicate machinery. And then I come home for peace and quiet and what do I find? Postman Magnuson's son in my cellar, the most notorious rascal of them all!"

Joachim felt cold all over. He wished he could die on the spot.

"Get out!" cried Gubben Janson flourishing the walking stick. And it was amazing how the stick, though it never touched him, helped Joachim scramble up the coal chute without any trouble.

When he escaped into the bright summer air, he ran right into his mother who was coming home to fetch another batch of cookies. Then Joachim wished he had never seen Gubben Janson's coal chute at all.

Chapter Ten

Bees

To Joachim the summer days seemed to drag. Ever since Midsummer Day he had felt out of sorts, partly because Mamma and Papa seemed always to look at him warily, but mostly because of Gubben Janson. Why did the old man act like that? If he had only talked to him, Joachim would never have needed to go into the cellar. He wasn't going to touch anything. He just wanted to learn. But Gubben Janson didn't care. He just shut himself up in his house. Joachim was angry. He went around muttering to himself.

Papa noticed Joachim's bad humor, and so did Karin and Greta. Joachim snapped at everyone. His black eyes flashed angrily at the world and especially at Gubben Janson and the old man's house.

One Saturday Papa brought Joachim a broken radio.

"Here," said Papa, smiling. "Maybe this will help cure whatever is wrong. You can take the whole thing apart."

Joachim looked at Papa and the radio in surprise. Papa had been different lately—wary, yes, but still different.

"Thank you," breathed Joachim, turning the radio wonderingly in his hand.

"Someone gave it to me," said Papa. "Go ahead and take it apart. Maybe you can fix it."

Joachim suddenly felt better. That afternoon he took the radio apart piece by piece. Papa came by Joachim's room, and there was a nice feeling in there.

But then Joachim couldn't fit the parts together. Although he worked hard to sort them into place, he didn't know what part belonged where. And though he patiently tried many ways, the radio would not go together properly. If only Olle were with him. Together they could surely do it.

When Papa came to help, he only made it worse. Papa had no feeling for machines.

"No, no," groaned Joachim. "You don't understand. That can't belong there. Don't you see the prongs can't go there?"

Papa sighed. "Have it your way." He left to read the paper.

Finally Joachim put the parts in a heap in an old box and shut the radio up in his closet. He stalked over to the window. Gubben Janson could have helped. Joachim glared at the house and felt miserable.

Days went by. On good ones Gubben Janson would come out every once in a while to fiddle with his beehives. Then Joachim would watch him from the window. One day he put wax in a hive, being careful to wear the net hat and the gloves. Joachim knew that was to help the bees make more honey. He had learned that in school. Usually bees produced their own wax to make the honeycombs. In the cells of the honeycomb they stored their honey, and that was also where the queen bee layed her eggs. By putting wax into the hive to be a foundation for the honeycomb, Gubben Janson could get more honey in less time.

One day he would have to take the old queen bee out and put a young one in instead, or else the bees would swarm out of the hives. If Gubben Janson forgot, the old queen would move away, taking most of the other bees with her, and then the hive would be left to the young queen and only the few bees that stayed with her.

Joachim knew all this from books. But he had never seen it, and the old familiar gnawing feeling was there. Joachim would have liked to know how those hives were made. But he was afraid to go look.

One hot day Joachim saw Gubben Janson carrying his smoke pot. That meant he was going to collect the honeycombs. The bees had to have room in the hive to make more honey or they would leave it.

Gubben Janson had bought new hives. They were not like

the old dome-shaped ones which made getting honey so hard. The new ones were metal with lids that lifted off. Since the bees built down from the roof, it was easier to get the honeycombs.

Joachim pressed his nose to his bedroom window and watched as Gubben Janson let the smoke from his pot drift into the hives. That stunned the bees. Then he carefully lifted the lids and took the honeycombs out. The bees were disturbed, and a few swarmed around Gubben Janson's net hat. But when the lids of

the hives went down again, they flew back into the hive.

Gubben Janson went into the house. Soon he was back with a large, lined basket. He put the honeycombs into it, and then went around the house, and Joachim could just see him walking off to the store to sell the honey.

Joachim looked longingly at the beehives. What was the use of just studying something in school when you could see the real thing? Besides, Gubben Janson was away, and Joachim didn't plan to touch anything. He would just peek and run right home. It wouldn't take a minute.

Joachim went into the living room. Greta was combing the hair of her precious doll, Karin had gone to the bakery for some reason or other, and his mother had gone to buy eggs from Mr. Kjellgren. The coast was clear. But what if someone caught him? What if . . . ? Joachim squared his shoulders. He wasn't going to be afraid. Besides, he wasn't doing anything terrible.

Quickly he went through the back door, past the berry patch, and up to the hives. The bees were buzzing. The sound was like the idling motor of the mail car, but much softer, and Joachim knew from school that the bees were fanning the hive inside with their busy wings. His teacher had said that was how the bees kept their home ventilated. Every so often a bee flew off to gather nectar, the sweet juice from flowers, which the bees used to make honey.

The humming grew louder. How was Joachim going to see how the bees fanned the hive unless he lifted the lid off? No.

That would be meddling with someone else's property. Just a quick look.

Joachim felt himself torn in pieces. Finally he couldn't stand it, and he lifted the lid. There was a row of bees facing inward, vibrating their wings. But Joachim didn't have time to see more because a bee stung him on the hand, and another stung him on his arm, and still another was settling on his forehead. He had forgotten to take a smoke pot.

"Owwww!" The stings hurt. Quickly Joachim snapped the lid down. It banged loudly, and Joachim looked up to see whether anyone had heard. And there . . . no, it couldn't be. But it was. There was Gubben Janson looking at him, standing by the corner of the house with his basket still full of honeycombs.

"So," he said as his eyes narrowed. "So you're at it again. You're no different from that child who broke my best clocks years ago."

Joachim looked away. His bee stings throbbed, and the blood beat in his ears. What Gubben Janson said wasn't true. It wasn't fair. Joachim closed his eyes.

"I'll teach you to stay away from my house," said the old man as he approached. "I happened to forget something I meant to take to the store. A good thing it was that I came back."

Joachim stood frozen. He watched as Gubben Janson came closer and closer. He couldn't move. He only stared with fright.

The walking stick whined and came down on one of Joachim's hands. That stung worse than the bee stings, but still Joachim

could not run away. It wasn't true. He would never have broken a clock. Swish! The walking stick rose above his other hand. Joachim trembled all over.

"Stop!"

Joachim spun around. There was Papa, home for lunch. He strode right up to old Gubben Janson. "What do you mean by striking my son?" asked Papa, and his voice was as cold as the block ice in the Magnusons' ancient refrigerator.

Gubben Janson lowered the walking stick. "He was into my bees," said the old man, "just as he's been into my cellar. Your son's curiosity is insatiable, and I mean to protect my property." Gubben Janson's face grew flushed.

"I appreciate your intentions," said Papa, drawing himself up with dignity.

Joachim stood with his mouth open while the bee sting on his forehead raised a handsome welt.

"But you have no right to strike my son," said Postman Magnuson. "He's my son, and I'm the one to punish him. I'll not have him the town's whipping boy."

Joachim stood dumbfounded. He could hardly believe his ears. Gubben Janson was also at a loss for words. Then the old man smiled a near toothless grin.

"Tsk, tsk," he said at last, shaking his head. "No, indeed, he'll not be the town's whipping boy. That child's a different breed from most. He's a bit like me," said Gubben Janson, and he laughed.

What did he mean? Joachim stiffened. He wasn't like Gubben Janson, was he? Surely the old man was joking? He couldn't mean that! Joachim turned to Papa. But Papa paid no attention.

"Look here, Mr. Janson," he said, "now that you are available, would it be too much to ask if you could have my watch fixed by next week? I need it, and it's been quite a while."

Gubben Janson frowned. "You can't rush these things. A watch is an intricate thing," he said. "It has to be examined thoroughly and appreciated. It has . . ."

"But I need it," said Papa impatiently. "Mrs. Grundling has been waiting for her clock far too long. I don't want to meddle, but you'll soon lose all the town's business if the work isn't done."

Gubben Janson's face grew dark. "Just because a man gets older he can't run his business his way, is that it? Well, good day then, sir!" Angrily the old man stalked off with his basket of honeycombs.

Then Papa turned toward Joachim. "Here it comes," thought Joachim. But Papa stood silent a while. "He's a stubborn old man," said Papa reflectively, "a very good craftsman, but it will do him no good at all. No one will want his skill. It happens like that sometime." Papa looked at Joachim. "He could get help and speed things up. But a person like him gets involved with things for their own sake. He forgets about the people. Then nothing can be done."

Joachim felt uncertain. This wasn't the way Papa usually acted.

"Let's look at those bee stings," said Papa and started for the house.

Joachim followed behind thoughtfully. It was such a puzzle. Everything seemed turned upside down.

In the kitchen Mamma looked up. She frowned at the lumpy sight of Joachim, but she quickly brought out the vinegar and swabbed the red lumps to draw out the poison.

"My, my," she said. "My, this must hurt. I didn't know you were so brave."

Joachim felt a little comforted. Then Greta, who was standing nearby, grew impish.

"Lump Lump!" she squealed. "Joachim is a Lump Lump."

"Stop teasing," said Papa.

Greta closed her mouth in surprise. For a minute Joachim felt like laughing at her funny expression, but the bee stings throbbed, and there was something troubling him more, something he had to think about.

Chapter Eleven

Papa Talks

Joachim went into his room and shut the door. For a moment he stood still. Papa had said something about Gubben Janson, that there was nothing to be done about him. Why was that? Joachim sat down at his desk and pressed a swab of vinegar-soaked cotton to his forehead.

Gubben Janson was in that house of his with all the tools, with the clocks and watches, with everything Joachim ever wanted. Gubben Janson knew about things that Joachim longed to know. What had Papa said? Gubben Janson forgot about people. That was certainly true. Joachim sighed. How often he and Olle had wished it were not so. And Gubben Janson didn't care a penny if his customers had to wait forever for their clocks and watches. That was why there was nothing to be done.

Joachim shut his eyes and tried to think. His stings ached. Through the window Joachim could just hear the whispering of the alders. Gubben Janson had said something too. He had said that Joachim was like him, a different breed from most. That couldn't be true, could it?

Joachim grimaced. He wasn't like Gubben Janson, was he? His lips felt dry. He stirred restlessly in his chair. One thing was certain, he didn't want to act like the old man. But when he had gone into the hen house, he'd forgotten about Mr. Kjellgren, hadn't he? That was only once, though. That didn't count. Joachim opened his eyes. When he'd gone into Gubben Janson's cellar, he'd forgotten about the old man. That didn't count either. The old man deserved it. What about Papa and the mail scale?

Joachim sat up straight. He would have to admit it. He had acted just like Gubben Janson. He had forgotten about people every time. Joachim sighed. Well, he would promise himself things would be different. From now on he was not going to act like the old man. From now on he would remember about people.

The trouble was that people never seemed to care about the feelings inside him, especially now with Olle away. It wasn't fair. Joachim was tired. The bee stings throbbed and ached. Why was Papa acting so differently? That was something he wanted to figure out too.

After a while Papa knocked on the door and came in.

"How are you feeling?" he asked.

"Better," said Joachim, still frowning.

Papa looked at Joachim. "What is it?" he asked.

Joachim picked at his insect collection on the desk. "I've been trying to think," he said. "I can't figure everything out."

"What can't you figure out?" asked Papa.

"Why you scolded Gubben Janson for hitting me. Why you didn't spank me. You've been acting so different with the radio and everything."

"Oh," said Papa and cleared his throat. He was silent for a while. "Well," he said at last, "this isn't easy for me, but I'm going to tell you something."

Joachim's black eyes fastened on Papa. He could see that it really was hard for Papa, and the discovery made him look down.

"I've been thinking a lot about what you said in the post office that day when you took the mail scale apart. You said that I didn't care. Well, it's true that I don't care as much as you do about how things work. But what you said bothered me. And I started thinking about it some more."

Joachim looked up. He watched Papa pacing up and down the room.

"You see, I do care a lot about many different things. I especially care about people. I like to listen to them. And it makes it nice for them, too, to come and tell me what is happening. It makes being postmaster interesting, maybe even meaningful."

Papa stopped pacing and looked at Joachim.

"But then, when I thought a long time about what you said, I began to see something. I began to see that you thought I cared about other people more than about you."

Joachim watched Papa carefully.

"It must have seemed to you that when people complained about you, I took their side and just punished you instead of trying to understand you and your side of the story first." Papa sighed. "Yes, maybe that was some of what I was doing. Parents can be wrong sometime, you know."

Joachim looked down. He'd never seen Papa this way. This wasn't pretend. He didn't know whether to laugh or cry. But he did know he had to tell Papa something too. He cleared his throat.

"Papa?"

"Yes, Joachim."

"I guess lately I've been so busy finding out things that I've just forgotten about people, the way you said about Gubben Janson. I guess we were both sort of wrong."

"I guess so," said Papa, and he rocked back and forth on the balls of his feet.

Chapter Twelve

Joachim Hears Things

Ever since the bee bites and Papa's talk, Joachim hadn't felt much like leaving the house. He still missed Olle a lot, but inside himself he was different. Now he fooled around with his stamp collection and minded Greta. He fixed a sprung hinge for his mother. But he didn't go anywhere.

The days were hot and muggy. There were big white cumulus clouds towering over the village. Mamma worried a little that Joachim wasn't getting out, that he didn't seem himself.

"You've been such a help to me lately in the house," she said, "but why don't you take the day off and go for a dip in Mr. Kjellgren's brook?" she suggested one day. "I asked him yesterday if you could, and he said yes. Run along. I'll fix you a sandwich to take with you."

Joachim hesitated. It was true, he hadn't had an excursion for a while. Maybe he should go.

"All right, Mamma," he said. And a little later, sandwich and bathing suit in hand, he went the ditch way past Gubben Janson's house.

Funny, Gubben Janson wasn't on the front porch. When it was warm like this, he always sat there. Oh, well. Joachim wasn't going to think about that. He wasn't going to get into trouble.

Mr. Kjellgren's brook was cool, and Joachim spent some time catching frogs and wallowing in the icy water. Long before noon he ate his meatloaf sandwich, and then he made a water wheel out of sticks and bits of string he had in his pocket.

He tied four twigs together at the middle like a star. And across the eight points he lashed smaller twigs to make eight paddles. Then he pushed a pin through the knot in the middle and stuck it into the end of a branch. The branch he balanced on a stone, leaving the wheel partly in the water. As the water rushed by the wheel, it turned gayly. He was pleased and would have stayed a long time, but a distant rumble warned him that it was going to rain.

Quickly he put his clothes on, and with his bathing suit dangling on a branch across his shoulder he set off for home. At Gubben Janson's house he ducked down in the ditch. Mrs. Grundling was banging on the door, mumbling something about her grandfather clock. Joachim stopped to watch. She rapped on the door sharply again.

"Mr. Janson," she called. "I know you are in there. I want to see you."

That was strange. Why didn't he come to the door?

Joachim hadn't time to wonder, because just then the first large drops of the promised shower fell heavily into the ditch. He hurried home, and out of the corner of his eye he saw Mrs. Grundling rushing toward her home before she too was caught in the shower.

The rain streamed down. Joachim went to his room to keep out of the way. Mamma was getting Greta ready to take to the city along with Karin. They were going with the mail car to town for new shoes. Soon the mail car swung up the road to the house to save the Magnusons a wet walk to the post office.

They called goodbye cheerily, and Joachim was left at home to fend for himself. What was he going to do? He went to the window. No, the shower wasn't going to let up for a long time yet. Joachim sighed. This was the kind of time when he had always gotten into trouble before. But he wasn't going to, not this time.

Then he heard something, a faint croaking like a crow. Funny. Generally birds did not sing in the rain. Oh, well, it was probably nothing at all.

There it was again. Kaw . . . kaw . . . kaw.

Joachim pretended not to hear it. He got busy with his insect collection, which he kept in assorted match boxes. Now, where had he put the cotton he needed to cushion his dragonfly? And where were the straight pins his mother had said he could borrow? He tried not to listen to the kaw, kawing, which turned into a rooster's crowing and then into a horse's whinny. The whinny was very unlike a horse, and Joachim felt sure something was wrong and that the crow and the rooster and the horse were one and the same voice. Not an animal voice but a human voice.

Joachim stood up. He couldn't keep his mind on the dragonfly on his desk. Who was making those strange noises? They were faint but . . .

Joachim drew on his black rubber boots and his slicker. He went out into the rain. He stood on the grass in front of the house.

"Kaw . . . kaw . . . kaw."

The sound came from the direction of Gubben Janson's house. Joachim approached carefully.

"Cock . . . doodle . . . do."

The sound was more distinct now. It was coming from the back of Gubben Janson's house.

"For heaven's sake . . . kaw . . . kaw . . . kaw."

Joachim heard. The voice sounded like Gubben Janson's, and it was weak. It came out of the coal chute opening. Joachim shuddered, thinking of the last time he had been there. He turned to go away.

"Someone help . . . cock . . . doodle . . . do . . . kaw . . . kaw," the voice went on hoarsely. It was little more than a whisper now.

Joachim stopped and bit his lip. He had to talk to himself now. Here he was with curiosity popping out all over his skin like measles. "Haven't you learned anything?" Joachim scolded himself. "You are ready to slide down the coal chute, just to be curious, aren't you?" he talked to himself crossly. "Well, I won't let you!"

Then the noise in the cellar stopped, and all Joachim heard was the pelting of the rain on his slicker. Hadn't he heard the voice say, "Someone help" . . . ? What if . . . what if . . . it was Gubben Janson who was hurt down there or maybe dead by now?

Joachim held his breath, and then in an instant he took off his slicker and stuck his booted feet through the coal chute. For a moment he was afraid. But he knew this time he was going down the coal chute not for Joachim Magnuson but because of whoever was calling down there. It took a moment for his eyes to adjust, and then he saw Gubben Janson sprawled out at the bottom of the rickety stairs with his left foot turned awkwardly under him.

"Joachim! Thank heavens you came," groaned the old man. "I thought I had scared you off for good."

"What happened?" asked Joachim breathlessly. "Are you all right, Mr. Janson?"

"Well not exactly," said Gubben Janson hoarsely. "I fell, banged my head. Must have, because all I remember is waking up to the rapping on the front door and then later the sound of a car going off. I've been making silly sounds down here ever since

because I knew that if you were home, you'd hear them, and then chances were your curiosity would bring you here. Only I was afraid I had scared you off for good. Run for help now. That's a good boy. The key to the kitchen door is in my coat pocket. Careful now."

Chapter Thirteen

Gubben Janson's House

And that was when Joachim finally saw the inside of Gubben Janson's house. He didn't stop to look really, though he caught a swift glimpse of tables full of watch parts—wheels and gears and little screws and tools. He ran for his father at the post office. And then they ran for the doctor.

It wasn't long before all three were back, and Gubben Janson was in his own bed with his left ankle taped securely.

"Stay off that foot now for a bit," said the doctor. "Your ankle is sprained and you need a good rest. Mr. Magnuson says his wife and the other ladies will take good care of you."

"Thank you," said Gubben Janson, "but about staying in bed . . . we'll see."

"If you don't, *you'll* see," said the doctor. "You can do some work in bed if you must. I'll come back and check up on you."

Then Gubben Janson groaned and looked miserable. But before everyone left, he motioned Mr. Magnuson to the bed.

"Would you take care of my bees until I'm up and about?" he whispered.

Papa nodded.

"And send that boy of yours over tomorrow, won't you? He's got itchy fingers, but he's all right."

Papa turned to Joachim and winked. Together they went home, stopping only to fetch Joachim's slicker at the back of Gubben Janson's house.

"Well now," said Papa once they were home, "Gubben Janson whispered something to me. It seems he wants you to go over to his house tomorrow. I wonder why?"

Papa didn't need to say any more. Joachim was grinning from ear to ear. Wait till Olle heard that!

The next day Joachim went to Gubben Janson's house. The door was wide open, and someone from the village had opened all the shutters. It felt so funny to walk right in. Joachim was a little afraid, but mostly from habit.

But once inside his eyes darted everywhere. The living room had two rockers and small tables full of watch parts. On the mantelpiece was a row of clocks, each ticking noisily to itself. An old radio stood on the floor with all its insides exposed. Why, there was even a mahogany music box on the sofa with a glass front so you could watch the machinery inside!

Joachim drew himself up. He mustn't dawdle. Gubben Janson was waiting. Quickly he went to the bedroom.

"There you are, Mr. Troublemaker himself," crowed the old man from the bed. "Have a look around now. A long one. I've guessed that you've been wanting to for a spell, and when you're through, you can bring the tray that's on the sofa over there. The tray with the tools and things on it. Don't touch anything else."

Joachim spent a blissful half hour looking around. There were clocks and parts of clocks in every nook and cranny of the house. Every table and every available chair had tools and gears on it. Joachim spent a long time by the music box, but he didn't touch it.

At last, when he had had his fill of looking, he brought the tray from the sofa to Gubben Janson. The old man smiled mischievously.

"Let's see if we can get some of that itch off your fingers," he said. "Maybe you could help me a bit. Seems everyone is fed up with me. That watch man in the city is getting extra business since my eyes started going bad."

Joachim looked flabbergasted. "You mean you want me to help you with the repairing?"

"What else? Keep you out of trouble, it will. There's got to be somebody with respect for delicate machines in this village. Besides, an old man like me gets lonely . . . not that I didn't bring it on myself." Gubben Janson cleared his throat. "All that crowing's made me hoarse," he mumbled. "Well, now, see

79

whether you can find the little screw by the place you wind the watch."

"But this is Papa's watch!" exclaimed Joachim.

"That's for a start, anyway. You want the mail to go out on time, don't you?" said Gubben Janson sternly. "Take the little screwdriver with the yellow handle. Let me see. Yes, that's the one. Go to it now. Mrs. Grundling isn't going to wait for her clock forever."

Joachim settled happily down near the bed. In front of him lay the tray of tools ready for work. They were beautiful. He felt somehow still inside and reverent. He'd never quite had that feeling before. Olle would never believe this. He could hardly believe it himself.

Joachim's fingers longed to get started. In a moment he plunged in and was lost in a world of gears and springs and screws, a world penetrated only by Gubben Janson's careful directions.

GUNILLA NORRIS was born in Argentina, the daughter of a Swedish diplomat. After World War II, the family moved to Sweden and eventually to New York, where English became their third language, although Swedish was always spoken at home. While studying at Sarah Lawrence College, the author met her husband, David A. Norris. They now live in Greenwich, Connecticut, and he is a minister at the First Presbyterian Church there. The Norrises have two children, Jennifer Anne and John Daniel. Mrs. Norris is the author of four other children's books, including *The Summer Pastures* and *A Feast of Light* for Knopf.

PAUL GIOVANOPOULOS was born in Greece and now lives in New York City. He studied at New York University and the School of Visual Arts and has exhibited his work throughout the United States and in several one-man shows. Mr. Giovanopoulos is the recipient of many awards, including the Society of Illustrators' Gold Medal in 1961. This is the eighth book he has illustrated for young people.

A Note on the Type

The text of this book was set in Linotype Palatino, a contemporary type designed in Germany in 1950 by Hermann Zapf. Modern type design occasionally reverts to the ancient Venetian masters for inspiration, and although this face bears the name of a famous penman of the sixteenth century, its design ranks it among Venetian romans, as is indicated by the broad design of the capitals and some of the lower case. Palatino is, nevertheless, an up-to-date, original type, not a mechanical copy of an historical type. Its elegance, weight, and cut-out appearance make it a particularly pleasing type face.

Typography by Karolina Harris